To Freddie
The hero of the story!

Freddie Panda and his friends are playing their best-loved game of roly poly.

It is lots of fun and much better than walking.

4

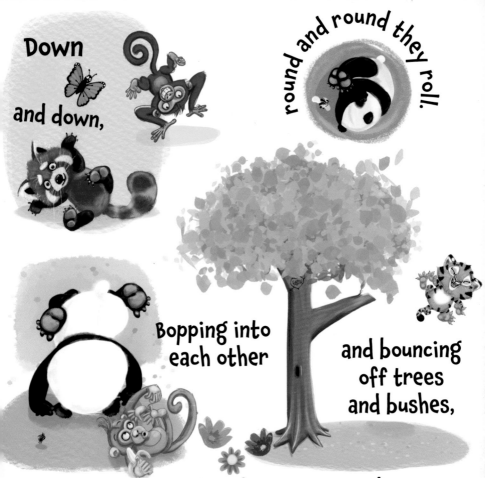

Down and down,

round and round they roll.

Bopping into each other

and bouncing off trees and bushes,

Pandas are so fluffy they never get hurt.

5

Suddenly –

SPLASH

they roll into an unexpected puddle of water.
Where has it come from? It hasn't been raining!

As they shake the water from their fur,

Freddie can see that the nearby river has burst its banks and he wonders why.

Freddie looks downstream and notices that the river is blocked with plastic bottles and other rubbish.

"Oh no!" exclaims Freddie "the water can't get through."

8

"We will have to remove the rubbish, or more of the jungle could be flooded. That would be a disaster for our friends and food supply." says Freddie. But how?

9

Freddie looks around
and sees his friend
Tumble is eating
some bamboo...

...and this
gives him
an idea.

10

Freddie asks Tumble to chomp down two long lengths of bamboo,

while he tears off strips from another piece and cleverly twists the strips into a net.

11

Working together the friends make an amazing makeshift bridge.

They wonder how to get it across the water.

"I know" says the tallest stretchiest monkey, waggling his floppy hands, "I can swing across!"

Using an extra long vine and taking an extra big leap...

12

...the monkey swings safely to the other side, landing like an acrobat.

Bit by bit, Freddie and his friends push the bamboo bridge across to him. The monkey stretches out his long arms and grabs the bridge, then using some vines he ties the bamboo bridge tightly to a nearby tree.

13

Freddie carefully shimmies out onto the bridge.
Being a bear, he's not
scared of climbing.

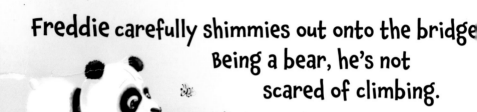

Just as he reaches the middle he loses
his grip and starts to slip!

Luckily he manages to
hang on with his strong
legs and sharp claws.
Dangling upside down,
he sees that he is
close to the rubbish
swirling in the water below.

inging on to the bridge, Freddie
egins scooping up the nasty
rubbish with the net.

15

The other jungle creatures all want to help, so Freddie passes the rubbish filled net to a monkey...

...who then gives it to the red panda...

...who finally hands it to the tiger!

The tiger empties the rubbish into one big pile.
"Why don't we call ourselves the Eco Crew,
as we are doing such a good job."
says the tiger. "That is a great idea."
says Freddie.

17

Finally, the last piece of rubbish is collected...

...and the river runs freely again. HOORAY!

Tumble the red panda
asks where the rubbish
came from.

Freddie
explains
that instead
of recycling it,

some people just throw their rubbish on
the ground and a lot of it ends up
in rivers and even in the SEA!

"That is terrible," says the red panda.
"We should remind everyone that -
If everybody does their bit
the planet will be fighting fit."

Freddie and the Eco Crew stand in front
of the big pile of rubbish, happy with
doing their bit to help.

The end